I0741951
IN MEMORIAM
107 DEAD
IN HOTEL
BLAZE—
MYSTERIOUS
ARSON SUSPECT

Frontispieces:

Ritual Wedding Triptych
Oil on Canvas, 1997

COCK ROBIN'S WEDDING

A HISTORY OF THE TRIALS OF EROS

(ACT I, Part 1)

Written and Illustrated by

Rebecca Migdal

Mythoprint Publishing
19 N. 14th Street
Easaton, PA 18042

COCK ROBIN'S WEDDING

A History of the Trials of Eros

Including a Dramatic
Re-Enactment of the Battle of the Sexes of the Gods

*As Told To His Scribe, Rosetta Stone
And Accompanied by a Particular Account, in Her Own Words,
of Fateful Meddling in the Affairs of Mortals.*

ACT I, Part 1

TABLE OF CONTENTS

Prelude One. *Arrival* *1*

Prelude Two. *In the Observatory* *11*

Prelude Three. *Reasons* *23*

Scene i. *Rosetta Sings a Duet* *27*

Scene ii. *Rosetta Dreams* *43*

Scene iii. *Robin Makes a Discovery* *59*

Scene iv. *Charlotte Receives a Present* *79*

Scene v. *Rosetta Awakes* *91*

Scene vi. *A Monster Aroused* *97*

Scene vii. *Rosetta Receives a Message* *103*

Scene viii. *The Tale of Asterion* *115*

Scene ix. *A Monster Unleashed* *127*

Prelude One.

Arrival

3
RLMIGDAL 5/2010

WELL, HERE WE ARE, MY LOVE...

WELCOME TO MY PALACE ON OLYMPUS!

WINCE!
MMF—

ROBIN...!
IT'S ALL RIGHT, CHARLOTTE.

WINCE!

SORRY.
MY FOOTMAN. HE'S, UH, SELECTIVELY DEAF.

TIME TO GET CHANGED, DARLING.

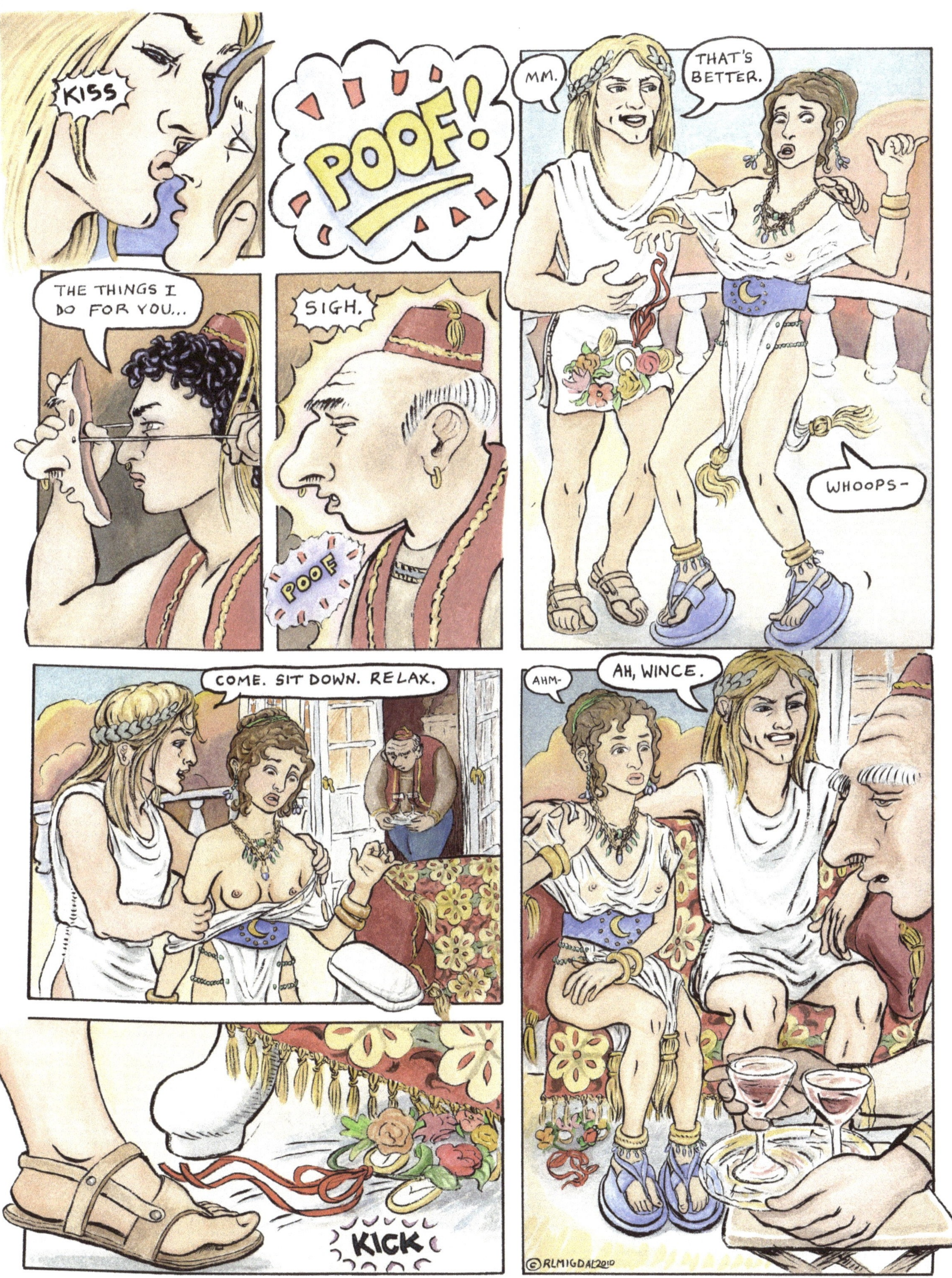

KISS
POOF!
MM.
THAT'S BETTER.
WHOOPS-
THE THINGS I DO FOR YOU...
SIGH.
POOF
COME. SIT DOWN. RELAX.
KICK
AHM-
AH, WINCE.
© RLMIGDAL 2010

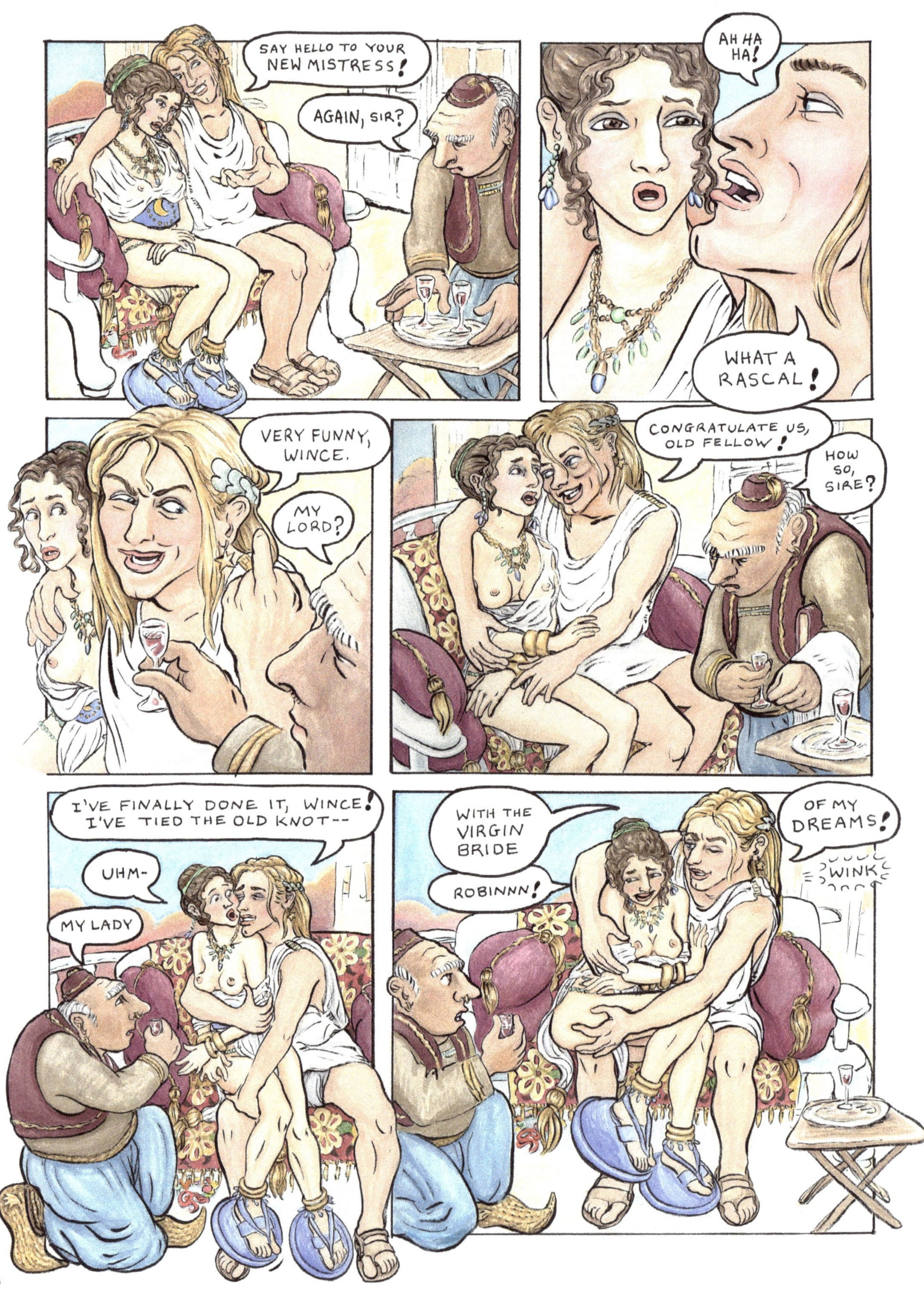

SAY HELLO TO YOUR NEW MISTRESS!
AGAIN, SIR?
AH HA HA!
WHAT A RASCAL!
VERY FUNNY, WINCE.
MY LORD?
CONGRATULATE US, OLD FELLOW!
HOW SO, SIRE?
I'VE FINALLY DONE IT, WINCE! I'VE TIED THE OLD KNOT--
UHM--
MY LADY
WITH THE VIRGIN BRIDE
ROBINNN!
OF MY DREAMS!
WINK

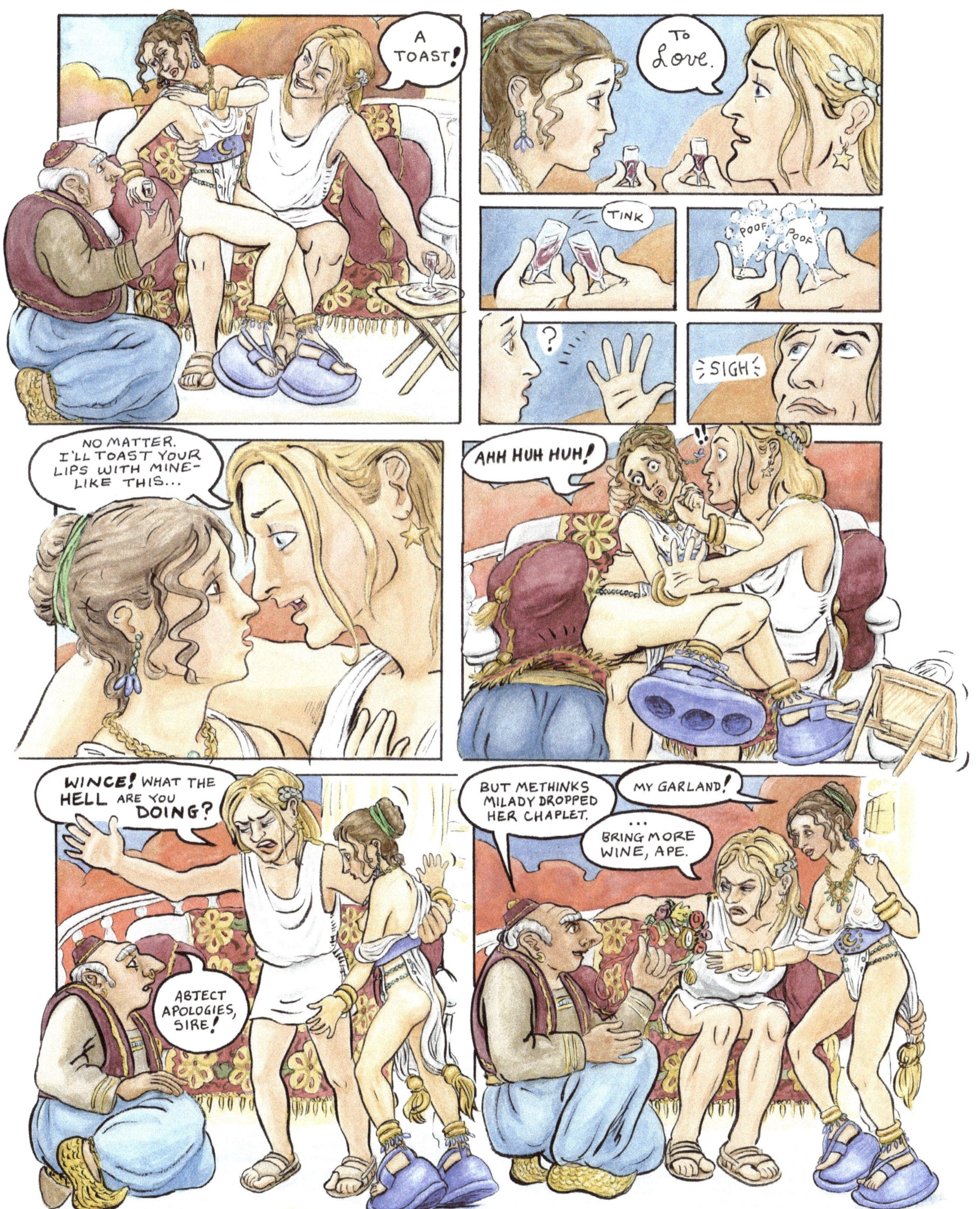

A TOAST!
TO Love.
TINK
POOF POOF
?
SIGH
NO MATTER. I'LL TOAST YOUR LIPS WITH MINE— LIKE THIS...
AHH HUH HUH!
WINCE! WHAT THE HELL ARE YOU DOING?
ABJECT APOLOGIES, SIRE!
BUT METHINKS MILADY DROPPED HER CHAPLET.
MY GARLAND!
...
BRING MORE WINE, APE.

AND NO MORE OF YOUR TRICKS!
YES, SIRE.
YOU MUSTN'T SHOUT AT HIM, LOVE -
POP
HE'S EVER SO GOOD...
YOU DON'T KNOW HIM, MADAM.
POP
:: KISS KISS :: YOUR LADYSHIP IS TOO KIND!
:: SLOBBER ::
:: SMOOCH ::
:: SMOOCH ::
BE OFF, LAMPREY!
ROBIN!
OOF!
YOWW!
LET GO!
WHAZZZ
OHO!
I'LL TAKE THAT—
HEY!
WHUUUMMMZZ
YIIIIPE!

Prelude Two.

In the Observatory

I know what you're thinking. How shameful! An innocent young woman has been seduced by a warlock prince, abducted to a palace in the clouds! Charlotte, a maiden barely more than a child, having fallen victim to the wiles of a reprehensible rake, struggles weakly in her captor's clutches, as he salivates in anticipation of her further defilement.

She has been carried to the house of one who has, admittedly, ruined more than one debutante. Her escape seems unlikely, for this is no ordinary crag, and it

won't be found in any tour book. It rises far higher than the Himalayas. Its roots cannot be traced on any map, nor are its peaks visible to mortals, nor to any living eye or mechanical device.

The fundament of Mount Olympos lies deep in the land of dream, where only sleepers wander, where madmen lose themselves, sometimes forever. The billowed heights of this awesome pinnacle rear up as far as the imagination can reach. From this altitude we gods look down upon the world of men and women, ever watching and listening, and meddling in the affairs of mortals.

For the Olympians take a keen interest in the doings of humankind. Their every thought and feeling, their every hope or despair, dream or fantasy, are of genuine concern to us. And so it should be, for without mortals we, the great eternal beings created in the image of women and men, would not exist, and from their dreams we find sustenance.

Here we see the palace of the mightiest of all the Olympians. These are the halls of Eros, bringer of life, quickener of the womb, secret driver of all exploits, master of desire. For you must know that the ever-youthful Cupid is the eldest of the gods.

Here the massive observatory where he sits and spies upon the hearts of all who feel the pricking of his poison darts. Here the endless chambers where his blessed favorites frolic. And here the catacombs where restless souls wander, seeking solace.

He is a busy god indeed!

The God of Love beckons even now. You have been permitted to enter his inner sanctum, where you are to be regaled with a history of his trials. For this tale is told at his command. It is his wish—my wish! For indeed, I am he! It is my wish... to explain my shameful deeds, in order to better understand the hurt they wrought upon me.

So I beg of you: listen, share my solace, and accept my gratitude. Ye mortals all, who daily curse my name, and ye fellow gods, gathered here in judgment! No doubt you assume that Charlotte, this delectable creature, is helpless to resist. Were her fate so sealed, there would be little here to tell. But the tale is long, for she is not what she seems.

Let me take you back, to review the circumstances leading up to the kidnapping of the delicious child, the abduction of Charlotte, the one true object of his desire.

Pardon the illeism. I must set this small distance between myself and the man I once was, the "he" that once was me. Perhaps even the God of Love may be transformed in a crucible of his own making, become more than what he was: a greater Self. Trials make men, they say... and gods too may suffer.

And now, on with the tale.

He sits at his console, a vast semicircular countertop that rings the observatory dome. The curving wall holds layer upon layer of glowing screens, and on their myriad surfaces flicker scenes from human lives, moments of desire, tenderness and desperation. When strung together, you call them love stories.

Normally his eyes take in one hundred lives per second, and his hands move quickly here and there, turning knobs and adjusting sliders. But just now the God of Love is neglecting his duties.

Eros is not alone in the cavernous dome. A small creature named Mammon scuttles here and there, searching for lost gold sequins, pearls and other articles of value. Mammon is one of the younger gods, taking the form of a pyramid with a single eye, a jagged gaping mouth, and wormlike tentacles. Here in the domain of Love he appears a tiny, mischievous fellow, but on earth below his aspect is gargantuan, and his prehensile limbs reach into every pocket and coffer.

Just now Mammon has found a scrap of gold foil that once decorated a bead at the throat of a celebrated Viennese harlot. This sliver of precious metal, shaken no doubt from the lace cravat of Eros, has found its way into the maw of the greedy idol.

"The vicar's balls," Mammon mutters happily. "Son of a scurvy baboon!" The deity of lust-for-wealth cannot speak except in profanities, but his vocabulary of these is encyclopedic.

The God of Love pays no heed. Rapt, he sits smoking a hand-rolled cigarette, and gazing in puzzlement at the lifestream of a single mortal. Her name is Rosetta Stone.

She stands, microphone in hand, on a cramped stage at one end of a long, narrow room. The musicians around her extract crashing and wailing noises from their instruments at a tremendous volume. With one finger in her ear, Rosetta belts out a quavering note. Her eyes squeeze shut for a moment, then she turns anxiously toward the man next to her, the one with the white guitar.

"What was that?" he barks.

A pale flash obscures the woman's form for a fraction of a second.

"There!" Eros adjusts a knob and something rather odd happens. Rosetta is in two places at once. It is as if we are looking at the dual images in a pair of binoculars, out of focus.

He runs the moment forward, and the woman divides like a cell. He nudges the slider and again watches the two figures resolve back into one, in slow motion. Then forward again: human meiosis.

"Ah!" The frozen image wavers on the screen. The doppelganger can clearly be seen diving into the crowd. She looks identical to Rosetta, but has short-cropped hair and is boyishly dressed. "Exactly the same as--"

The god adjusts the coordinates on a nearby screen, bringing up an urban landscape lit by street lamps and the headlights of vehicles. A figure strides quickly across the broad intersection and as a car approaches, we see her stormy, tear-streaked face. It is Rosetta's doppelganger, hastening away from the scene of her birth.

"But where is she going?" As the figure melts into the darkness, Eros reaches for his glass of wine and takes a thoughtful sip. "She simply vanishes!"

"Pretty caught up in this one, eh Robin?"

Eros turns with a guilty start. "Wince! I didn't hear you come in."

Bagoas Wince, better known as the god Hermes, advances wielding a covered dinner plate, a cloth draped over his arm. The god Eros, a. k. a. Cock Robin, turns back to his console, brings his cigarette to his lips.

"It's an interesting case," he remarks. "Look at this: here she becomes upset, and here she suddenly splits off, creating a second personality. Literally an evil twin!"

Wince meanwhile shakes out the cloth, manifesting a lit candelabrum and various utensils.

"A chick singer with a phantom evil twin?" he chuckles. "You must be smitten then."

"Fuck you," Robin retorts fondly, leaping down from his magic carpet. Wince sets the platter down on the tablecloth, which floats in the air, rigid.

"Luncheon is served!" he intones, lifting the lid to reveal his masterpiece. "Voilà! Salmon soufflé à la teton, with potato cockettes."

Robin gazes in surprise at the feast.

"You... you shouldn't have, Wince. And yet..."

"I always do," Hermes responds cheerfully. "Will you at least taste it, my lord?"

"You know I don't really eat." Eros reaches up to put his arms around the neck of the taller god. "Pearls before swine, I'm afraid."

The two men kiss.

Let us turn our attention to the console behind them. As the population of humans grew, it became essential for Eros to construct an administrative device, and this one has proved adequate until quite recently. It is a handsome piece of furniture, designed and maintained by the Swiss inventor Jost Bürgi, who after his death in 1632 entered the service of the Olympians.

Each of its hundred or so monitors has its own identical set of controls, simple enough in their meaning and function. To the left is a switch labeled "leben" above and "sweven" below; that is, "to live" and "to dream". This switch then enables the god to choose whether he will enter into the waking or the sleeping thoughts of the subject. To the right of this are four small dials. Each one controls a range of strong emotions: anger, sorrow, regret and jealousy at the one extreme, and at the other, tenderness, joy, hope and pride.

To the right of the dials are three sliding knobs. These set the coordinates used in targeting the wretched mortal whose happiness is at stake. The first sets the coordinates in space, the second in time, and the third in the realm of the spirit: the fifth dimension, as it were.

There are no wires or circuits within the ebony cabinetry. The knobs and dials are not connected to any known machinery. The console is merely a physical representation meant to channel and organize the god's innate magical properties. The entire function of this display is record-keeping: to enable him to track the details of multiple investigations.

But we are neglecting the large dial to the right, the most important of all. This dial of course controls the level of desire in the subject, the default being indifference, with settings ranging from repugnance to raging lust.

Hermes is on his knees now, kissing the hands of his lord and beloved. He is transported with gratitude, for Eros has commanded him to prepare a bath in the royal thermae for their mutual enjoyment.

Wince rises and departs in happy haste. Robin returns to his console and summons up another sequence from the past. It is a scene from the inner life of the mortal woman Rosetta, as described in the journal she keeps to record her dreams.

I dreamed I was back on Nesbit Street.
The walls of the house still echoed with
Mom's shrieks of rage.

I went into the kitchen.
She was cleaning cat shit off of the lino-
leum floor with her bare hands.

I walked into the dining room.
Right at the spot where I once found Silky eating my pet mouse...

I got this weird, horrible feeling.
I was vibrating like a gong, and there was a ringing in my ears.

Suddenly, there was ANOTHER ME standing a few feet away!

She lounged against the wall, glaring at me .

I was horrified at the thought of kissing her.

As the two Rosettas' lips meet, something unheard-of occurs in Robin's observatory. All the monitors begin to display the same scene at once! Over and over again, one Rosetta kisses the other, and the two become one.

The observatory of Eros echoes with the hum of the woman becoming, at least temporarily, whole.

"I'll get to the bottom of this!" Eros cries, mounting his magic carpet with a bound.

Mammon has somehow found his way onto the carpet!

"Yiiiii!"

Robin's tender parts have been lacerated by the pyramidal imp's pointed summit.

Seizing the material god with both hands, Robin sends him sailing in a broad arc above the marble floors of vitreous pink.

"Puck's pubes!" howls Mammon, waving his tentacles. "Leprous ta-" His curses are truncated by a satisfying crunch, and the clatter of falling bricks.

Let us now leave Eros and Mammon to nurse their wounds and perpetuate their eternal feud. We turn to the world of mortals, and to Rosetta Stone, who has captured the interest of the God of Love.

Prelude Three.

Reasons

Reason number five: bad coffee. Cheap, generic drip blend, brewed weak with scalding water, tasting of paper and well chlorinated. If you take it light, your sole recourse is lumpy creamer that leaves a gelatinous oil slick on the surface as the vile mixture cools.

Reason number four: Greg from New Jersey. Greg with his stupid smirk, his virginal mustache and his Howard Stern habit. Yesterday he staggered into my desk as he walked by, leered and said "ex-squeeze me!"

Ex-squeeze me, huh? He'll be lurching up against me in the elevator next.

Reason number three: this letter I'm supposed to be composing. About how abortion is murder, and the Right to Life must be defended, so please give generously to the Bob Jones fund for wayward girls. Do it for Jesus!

Then it's more begging letters to old ladies on behalf of the Sisters of Mercy, or Saint Francis Xavier... and on every envelope and reply card, a little picture of the saint. Good ole Francis Xavier, who tortured and burned thousands during the Inquisition in Goa.

I think I'm breaking out in hives, getting a nasty rash. Or maybe it's pink-eye. Something is definitely wrong with me. Plus I have sinus problems, and I wake up with migraines (which explains my desperation for caffeine in any form, no matter how loathsome.) Anyway it's interfering with my singing. That's reason number two.

It was pretty weird when I found out that the boss, Mr. Wrigley, has multiple sclerosis. I've never seen him stumble, never heard his speech slur. Peggy over in sales said it's because when an episode starts, he just goes and gets all his blood changed for fresh, clean plasma.

See, MS is like having a fascist police state inside your body. Nazi white blood cells patrol your bloodstream following deranged orders: to identify 'enemy' nerve cells, attack and destroy. A military coup of the immune system against the intelligentsia, MS spawns vast lesions on the brain.

But apparently not Mr. Wrigley's brain. Guess he can afford a 100% blood transfusion whenever he needs one.

Cyndi, on the other hand, was living on social security. The state-approved treatment for MS: massive doses of steroids.

Steroids. Jesus. That shit will mess you up. For all the good it did...

Cyndi was easily the coolest kid in our family, our daring leader. She's the one who taught us to sing in four-part harmonies.

She spent the last five years of her short life in a wheelchair.

And here I am, wasting my prime... drawing sanctimonious portraits of mass murderers.

Ha, ha. A little genocide is all it takes, to get candles lit in front of your statue. Cyndi would have laughed at that one.

Well little big sister, this ain't my idea of a promising career path, either.

So that's reason number one.

I haven't told Enoch yet. I hope he doesn't get too mad...

5 Reasons
to Quit
My Job

Scene i.

In Which Rosetta Sings a Duet

Rosetta Stone
2008 RLMIGDAL

New York City, 1996

Enoch and I were still together back then...

AKA BAR

DON'T DENY YOURSELF...

WINDUP TEETH

UP TO 11

EXIT

LIKE HELL I WILL, ASSHOLE!

HEY.

...and so were The Windup Teeth, the band we forged when we met in '90.

Being a rock star was Enoch's only dream. Music, then, was the path to winning and keeping his love.

I'd been working for a over year at a design firm, so I had money to spend on my man.

THIS IS THE LAST TIME I'LL EVER SEE YOU. YOU'RE LYING IN BED
AND YOUR HAIR IS SPREAD OUT ON THE PILLOW...
IN A SOFT BLACK BILLOW LIKE THE WINGS OF A LOON.

THIS IS THE LAST TIME
I'LL EVER KISS YOU.
AND I WAS REALLY HOPIN'
THAT BEFORE WE GO
YOU'D OPEN
ONE CHINA-BLUE EYE.
'CUZ WE HAFTA SAY
GOODBYE.

AND YOU OPEN UP TWO.

AND I GUESS I KNEW
THIS WAS THE LAST TIME
I'D EVER REALLY SEE YOU.

I'D LIKE TO SAY
IF IT WAS JUST ME
I'D TOSS THE GAME AWAY
JUST TO STAY WITH YOU.
BUT EYELIDS OF STONE
SINK UNDER SLUMBER
YOU'RE DRIFTING DOWN
ALONE...
OH...
Sparkler......

SO WE GET INTO THE VAN
AND DRIVE UNTIL IT'S NIGHT
TO WHERE THE CHILDREN STAND
SOMEONE IS WAITING FOR
A LIGHT
WITH A SPARKLER
IN HER HAND

OH HOW SHE SPARKLES
UP IN THE SKY
OUT IN THE DARK
SEE THAT SPARK?
WATCH HER FLY...

THROW YOUR SPARKLER UP IN THE SKY...
LET HER FLY
I COULDN'T EVEN HEAR MYSELF UP THERE!
TAKE A POWDER, ROSETTA. WHAT'S YOUR PROBLEM?
BACK STAGE
OH, FOR GOD'S SAKE.
SNORK
SOB
SHE JUST LOST HER SISTER, MAN! YOU'VE GOTTA TAKE CARE OF HER!
I SOUNDED TERRIBLE!

Meanwhile, at Rosetta and Enoch's apartment...
ARRRGH. TWO!
HEH, HEH! THE GOB- LINS ARE CLOSING IN!

HA! THE ZOMBIE GETS FIVE! —AND, USES FREEZE FORCE ON LOTHAR the GREAT.
NOOOOOOOOOOOOOO

THE TRAP DOOR IS LOCKED!
THERE'S NO ESCAPE!

LATER ...
THANKS!
ANTOINE IS A GREAT KID! WE HAD SO MUCH FUN. —CALL ME ANY TIME.

Scene ii.

In Which Rosetta Dreams

CYNDI STONE 1959-1995
CYNDI STONE 1959-1995
SHE'S GONE...
I awakened, muttering, from deathly dreams...

ENOCH? - SNIF.
Then I fell asleep again, to dream a dream...
SNIF
that would change my life forever.
WHO IS IT?

January 27th, 1996

I and a male friend are trying to sleuth out the reasons for the destructive fire. It turns out that the tenant on the top floor is author Charlotte Eyre- a recluse and an invalid. We want to know how the fire started and if it had anything to do with her.

The young man goes back in time to pay a visit to the unhappy recluse before the fire. He is a longtime admirer of her work. He becomes her friend-her only friend.

She has been alone so long, worrying the canker of her disillusioned love. An amnesiac old woman (though she is still surprisingly young-looking) who no longer writes. She barely even leaves her chair.

I watch myself play both roles: the admiring young friend, and the pale old maid, the embittered muse of romance.

The youth and I are looking through Charlotte's papers, hoping for a clue.

There are old documents relating to a Bill or William Norton, the host of the restaurant and hotel below. We learn that Bill rejected Charlotte because her profession as an author made the match unacceptable to his family. He is the man who is responsible for Charlotte's disappointment.

We discover a painting of him on the wall.

"He looks exactly like Enoch!" I remark. Although Bill is certainly hand-some, his charming expression has more than a trace of arrogance.

There is another mystery afoot in the doomed old house. A small child has become inappropriately initiated into sexual matters, and is developing some strange relationships with the guests.

My avatar and I are still examining the contents of Charlotte's room. We find that although she stopped writing and published nothing during her reclusive years, she did produce a few drawings, and very strange ones indeed.

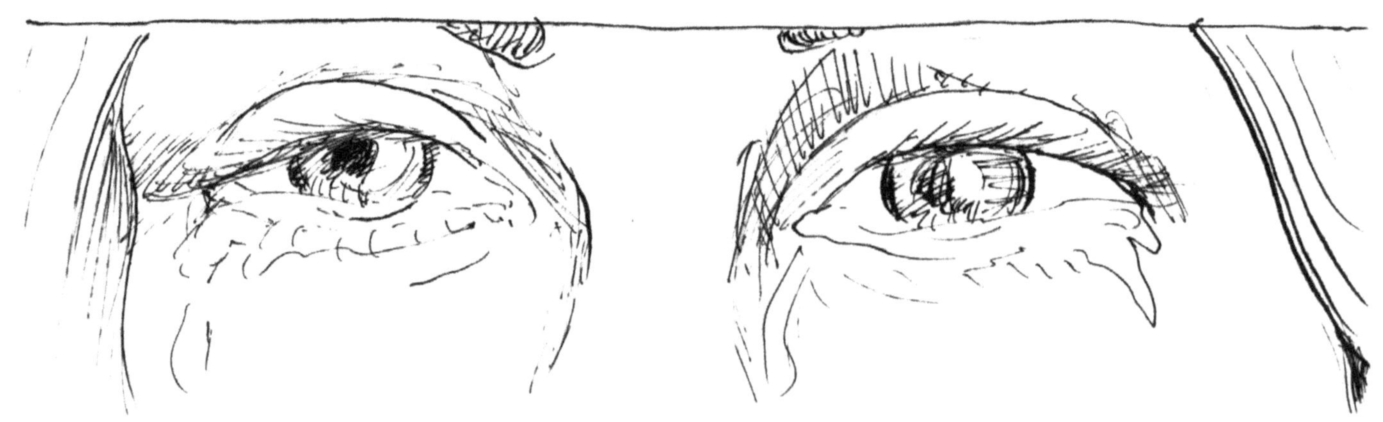

How dare you! What can your intentions have been? not only for the loss insult
...must be... Our acquaintance severed comeplete Mr. Norton!
was killed in a terrible fire, leaving all his WORLDLY POSSESSIONS TO CHARLOTTE E F.
IT SAYS HERE THAT BILL DIED IN 1855.
OH WELL.
I NEVER DID LIKE THE GUY ALL THAT MUCH.
BOO HOO HOO HOOO...
It's my fault... it's all my fault!

One very large drawing is of an oddly deformed hippopotamus. It's a "cutaway" medical view of the hippo. Along the bottom edge are sections of the legs, tail, mouth and anus. Where the head should be, there's nothing. The mouth is placed below the neck, with an ear on one side and the anus on the other. The top half of the hippo is simply a huge rectangle of cells, squarish segments with different colored, bordered areas delineating zones carefully marked and somehow cerebral, spiritual, conceptual.

This is a very messed-up animal, we conclude.

The young man returns often to visit Charlotte. He wants to make up for her loss, grief and disappointment. He both pities and admires her, and he takes this for love, because it makes his regard for her feel heroic. Sweeping past her frosty, pained reserve, he "makes love" to her, describing himself as her "ardent admirer". She pulls away coyly, but is clearly affected and shaken. She has clung so long to her monumental isolation. Her spirit within its frozen shell is weak and insecure.

She is not in her room now, but making her way back toward it through a throng of people. She is returning from the bathroom, feeling shy, embarrassed, and strange at being among people for the first time in so many years.

Just as she mounts the stairs that surround the central hall, a speaker takes the podium and begins to introduce his topic. He is annoyed that so many people are still moving about. He is broad-faced, sandy-haired, intellectual of countenance.

"Those of you who feel that they must use the bathroom during breaks, please be sure to allow enough time to return to your seats before the presentation resumes," he says in a faintly British accent. It seems to Charlotte that he is looking directly at her. Horrified with chagrin, she hastens back toward her room. On the landing a vision appears: fierce tongues of flame issuing from her room, destroying everything in their path. It must have been she who lit the fire in her self-destructive frenzy!

Or was it?

Charlotte arrives at the door to her room. There are two young girls there, the elder of them about ten years old. They are scantily dressed and giggle as she opens the door.

There is a shirtless blond youth reclining beside the door. He is very young, with long hair and the face of a lovely woman. Charlotte thinks his expression cold, hard, passionate without object.

"I'm here to collect on the promise you made me," he states. "You said you'd marry me."

Charlotte is moved by his great beauty. She strokes his cheek and says, "Oh, but you're too young." She cannot take him seriously.

"But you promised, don't you remember?" he says flatly. There is no question in his eyes, only the certainty that this thing will happen.

"I said yes?" Charlotte gasps. The door is still open, and the two girls are watching and listening.

Charlotte fans herself with her hands, feeling faint.

(It seems to me that I am playing the part of Charlotte extraordinarily well, almost as if it were really happening.)

OH MY-
FLAMES!

OH—I
THOUGHT—

THIS WAS MY ROOM...
I'M HERE TO COLLECT ON THE PROMISE YOU MADE ME.
YOU SAID YOU'D MARRY ME.
OH... NO. YOU'RE TOO YOUNG.
BUT YOU PROMISED.
DON'T YOU REMEMBER?
I SAID YES?
OH, MERCY!

Scene iii.

In Which Robin Makes a Discovery

MON DIEU!
OH, LALA!
RRRRRR
SUCK

RRRRRRRRRRRR
SUCK
OH!
BETTY! —JIM!?
GROWOOOO!
NOT NOW, MAMMON!
CLUMP!

WHO IS IT?
ROOG!
HOW COULD YOU?
I WAS WATCH-ING THAT—

WE'RE INTER-VIEWING THE OLDER RESIDENTS—
WHAT IN THE NAME OF HADES—!!

WE'RE INVESTIGATING A TERRIBLE FIRE.
WELL. I'M CERTAINLY OLD.
COME IN.

WHO ARE YOU?
BANG
BANG
MMNG! GGRG!
LEBEN
SWEVEN
LEBEN

MY—MY NAME IS CHARLOTTE EYRE. I'M AN AUTHOR—
AHA.
LEBEN
SWEVEN
CLIC

I'VE BEEN VERY ILL FOR A LONG TIME, AND I LOST MY MEMORY—OR SO I'M TOLD.
IT'S HER DREAM... OH—OF COURSE! SHE'S ONE OF MY PRISMATIC LOVE NODES...WHICH CAN ONLY MEAN—

CHARLOTTE EYRE—?
ICE
LEBEN
SWE
LEBEN
SWEVEN
THAT BEARDED ME IS NO MERE DREAM SPRITE, MAMMON!

WOW. I'VE READ EVERY SINGLE ONE OF YOUR BOOKS.
Charlotte
CLEARLY SHE'S BEEN VISITED BY A ROGUE AVATAR

IT'S REALLY YOU!
THE BOW AND ARROWS... THAT BREASTPLATE! I'D KNOW THAT OWL BREASTPLATE ANYWHERE.

SO.
I'VE FOUND YOU AT LAST.

OLYMPIC
SUPER SPONGE
SUCKING Mermaids
FOUR FLAVORS!
MARA SIOUXIE FIONA PHAEDRA
EXPANDING
♪♫

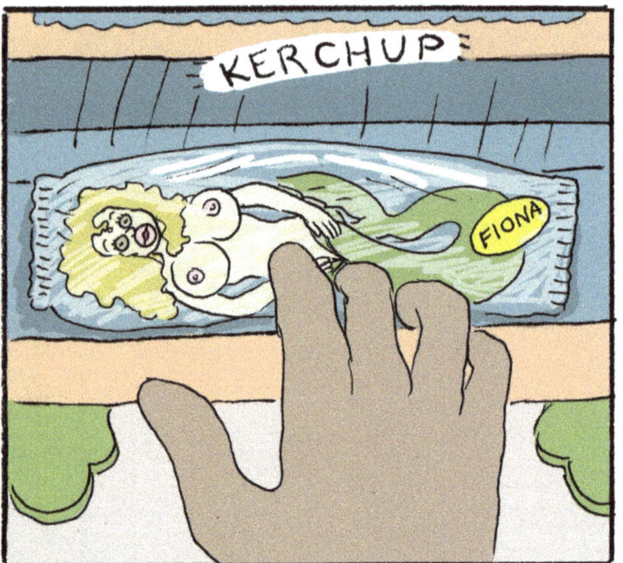

KERCHUP
FIONA

FFFIZZZZZZZZZZZZZ

SORRY GIRLS, NO MUSES REQUIRED. NOW SHOO!
'210 DVEIN BLAZE

WILLIAM DIED IN THE FIRE...
LOOK AT HER! SHE'S TRAPPED IN AN INFINITE REGRET LOOP!
DEFINITELY AN ADVANCED CASE OF THE ROT.
TAKE IT EASY, DARLING!! I'M GETTING YOU OUT OF THERE.
MAYBE I CAN REACH HER IN ETERNITY MODE.
OK. GOT 'ER.
YUP. SHE'S FROZEN IN ETERNITY.
BRRRRR! FIRST OFF, I'LL HEAT THINGS UP A BIT—
BURNING
HOT
WARM
TEPID
COOL
COLD
FREEZING
THAT'S RIGHT, SWEETHEART.
TAKE IT OFF.
TAKE IT ALL OFF.
SO...
HOT...

OH, COME ON!
IT'S 101 DEGREES IN THERE...
LUST IS SET AT MAXIMUM...
AND SHE'S STILL IN HER NIGHTIE!
WHY IS SHE SO RESISTANT?

ARRGH.
WONDER WHAT'S GOING ON IN DREAMLAND...

NO, BILL!
CHARLOTTE— I BEG OF YOU!
OK— IT LOOKS LIKE SHE'S RELIVING THE TRAUMA THAT SENT HER OVER THE EDGE.

THERE'S BEARDED ME AND THAT MORTAL GIRL... WHAT WAS HER NAME? ROSETTA. KINDA HOT, AND A FINE DREAMER.

IF IT WASN'T FOR HER, I MIGHT NOT HAVE FOUND DIANA IN TIME TO SAVE HER.
I MUST HAVE WINCE SEND HER A TOKEN OF MY FAVOR.

ARE YOU TAKING THIS DOWN, MAMMON?
%*@&#!!
GOOD.
%@#!
$$

BATH TOYS, FLUFFY TOWELS, CHAMPAGNE, CHOCOLATES...

PERFECT!

IT'S ALL MY FAULT...

IT'S JUST NOT WORKING! IS SHE TOO FAR GONE?
NO! I WON'T LET ARTEMIS FADE AWAY!
EVEN IF I HAVE TO USE...

THE COSMIC BOW!
I SWORE TO PSYCHE THAT I'D NEVER EMPLOY YOU AGAIN ON A MORTAL...

BUT MY QUARRY ISN'T HUMAN.

OKAY... I'VE GOT A LOCK ON 'ER.
JUST LOOK AT THAT THREE-WAY FEEDBACK!
KCHUK
LUST
DESIRE
SPARKS
ACTION
CLIC
FUCK! I'M LOSING HER!
OFF
BOLT MODE
ZZONNGG
uuhhhhoOOM!

zomm mmmmmm
Zzzzzzakk
OHHHHH SHIIIIIIIIIIT!
Zzzziff

RAAHBINN... YOUR BATH IS—

ROBIN?

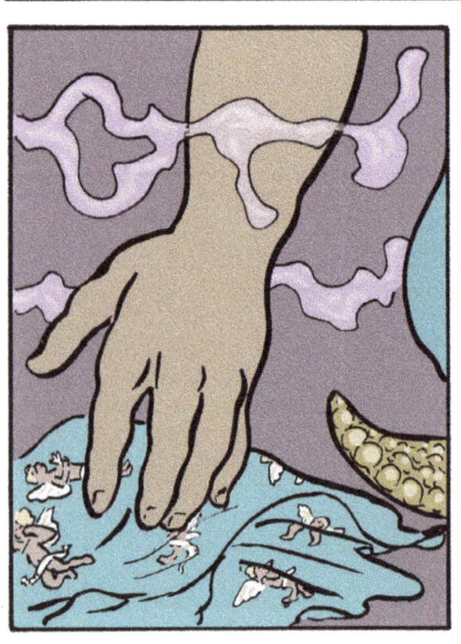

SIGH

whooom

REFLECTION IN A TEASPOON...
I'M STIRRING MY CUP...

AND WHAT WOULD YOU TASTE LIKE...
CHARLOTTE... CHARLOTTE!

IF I DRANK YOU UP?
EYES LIKE AN OWL'S GAZE INTO TIMELESS REGIONS...

SCARS FORMING RIDGES THAT CLOSE OVER LESIONS.
CHARLOTTE. ARTEMIS!

IT'S ME!
YOU WORRY A CANKER OF LONG DISILLUSION...

YOUR MIND IS A BLANKET— YOUR HEART A CONTUSION!
OH, GOD!

WE'RE
SO
ALIKE,
YOU AND I...

WHOOM
CHARLOTTE EYRE.

MONUMENTAL
CHILD
DIVINE IN YOUR
MADNESS,

WOULD MY
TENDER KISS

BE A
BALM
ON YOUR
SADNESS?

MY LONGING YAWNS WIDE,
A WILD ABYSS CALLING...

OH LET ME FALL WITH YOU
WHEREVER YOU'RE FALLING...

FALL TO ME... —CALL TO YOU!

CHARLOTTE EYRE.

GASP

(— SOB —)

SHAFT OF LIGHT

PENETRATE

THE DARK, TURGID CLOUD

WRAPPED WELL ABOUT THEE
MORE THICK THAN A SHROUD.

THE GAZELLE STANDEST TREMBLING

TOO LATE NOW, HE COMES:
THE SCENT OF THE HUNTER...
THE SWALLOWING DRUMS...
BUM BUBBITY BUM
BUM BUM

RUN NOW INTO DANGER
A SNARE-TRIPPING WIRE,
THE NET'S IN THE CHASM
I AM HERE, THOU GAZELLE
I AM HERE,
I AM HERE!
THE PIT IS ON FIRE.
TASTE THY FEAR, SAVOR WELL
THOU TREMBLING GAZELLE...
THOU TREMBLING GAZELLE...

MEANWHILE, THE MONITORS ALONG THE WALLS OF THE OBSERVATORY HAVE GONE STRANGELY DARK.
UH-OH. I HOPE ROBIN'S OKAY!

@×✳~✂!
MMRROOUFF!

MROOWRGH!
MAMMON!
A MESSAGE? FROM ROBIN?

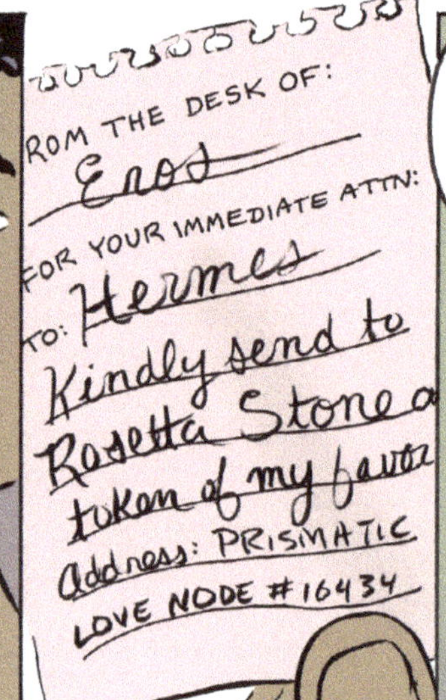

ROM THE DESK OF:
Eros
FOR YOUR IMMEDIATE ATTN:
TO: Hermes
Kindly send to Rosetta Stone a token of my favor
Address: PRISMATIC LOVE NODE #16434

⊰SIGH⊱ WHY I PUT UP WITH HIS SELFISHNESS I'LL NEVER--
PLINK PLONK

#426. MAGIC WREATH
Safe! Effective!
True Love Forever
by Olympic Charms
EFFECTS: FIND YOUR TRUE LOVE plus RESTORE LOST MEMORIES
• GUARANTEED TO WORK ON MORTALS. NOT YET TESTED ON IMMORTALS. SEE LEGAL DISCLAIMER.
HUH!
LOOK AT THIS. WOULDN'T IT BE A LAUGH IF I--
WAIT A SEC. WHAT IF I DID?
HE'D KILL ME! HEE HEE.
BUT HE DOESN'T HAVE TO KNOW.
OH, THIS IS GOOD... "REQUEST THIS TOKEN ON BEHALF OF EROS. EMISSARY: THE GODDESS NUT." AND SEND.
PLOMP
HAH! FLING OVER.

Scene iv.

In Which Charlotte Receives a Present

The youth pulls out a large and wickedly sharp knife and carefully draws it along the pad of her thumb, just enough to cut the upper layer of the skin and cause a slight sting, but drawing no blood. It is clear that this "marriage" is to be a rape. Charlotte, a virginal old maid, feels her command of herself snap as if she were a puppet whose strings had been cut!

She looks at the boy, fascinated and frightened by what she realizes is a supernatural quality about him. He surely has powers beyond that of a mortal, she thinks, and this is no ordinary rape, but a ritual wedding commanded by some power that operates largely unseen, incarnate now in the form of this man/woman/boy.

And yet he is also a victim, she is sure: a sore spot, an eruption from the lesion on the underside of human-ity, a force arisen out of the collective pain. He is the child prostitute, drug addict and porn plaything, whose powers are infused out of others' desire, while he feels none: act-ing out the fantasies of others, lit in a godlike radiance.

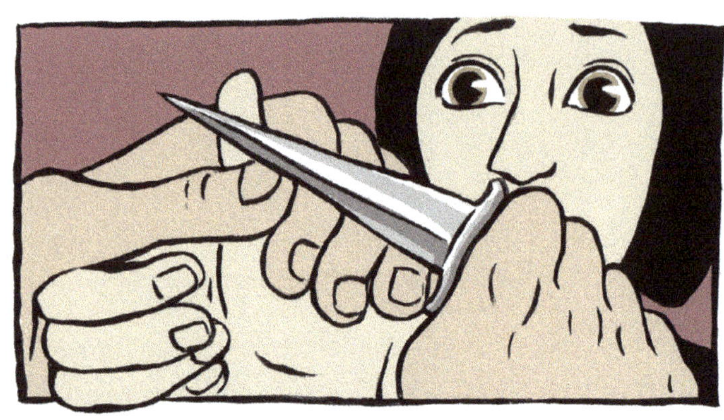

HMPH.
NO BLOOD.

IS THIS SOME KIND OF RITUAL WEDDING?

WHO ART THOU, SULLEN ANGEL,
WITH RAZOR-EDGED WINGS? THOU BOY HARLOT POUTING, ADDICT AND PLAYTHING...
THOU CONSTRUCT OF PAIN, THOU DARK INCARNATION—

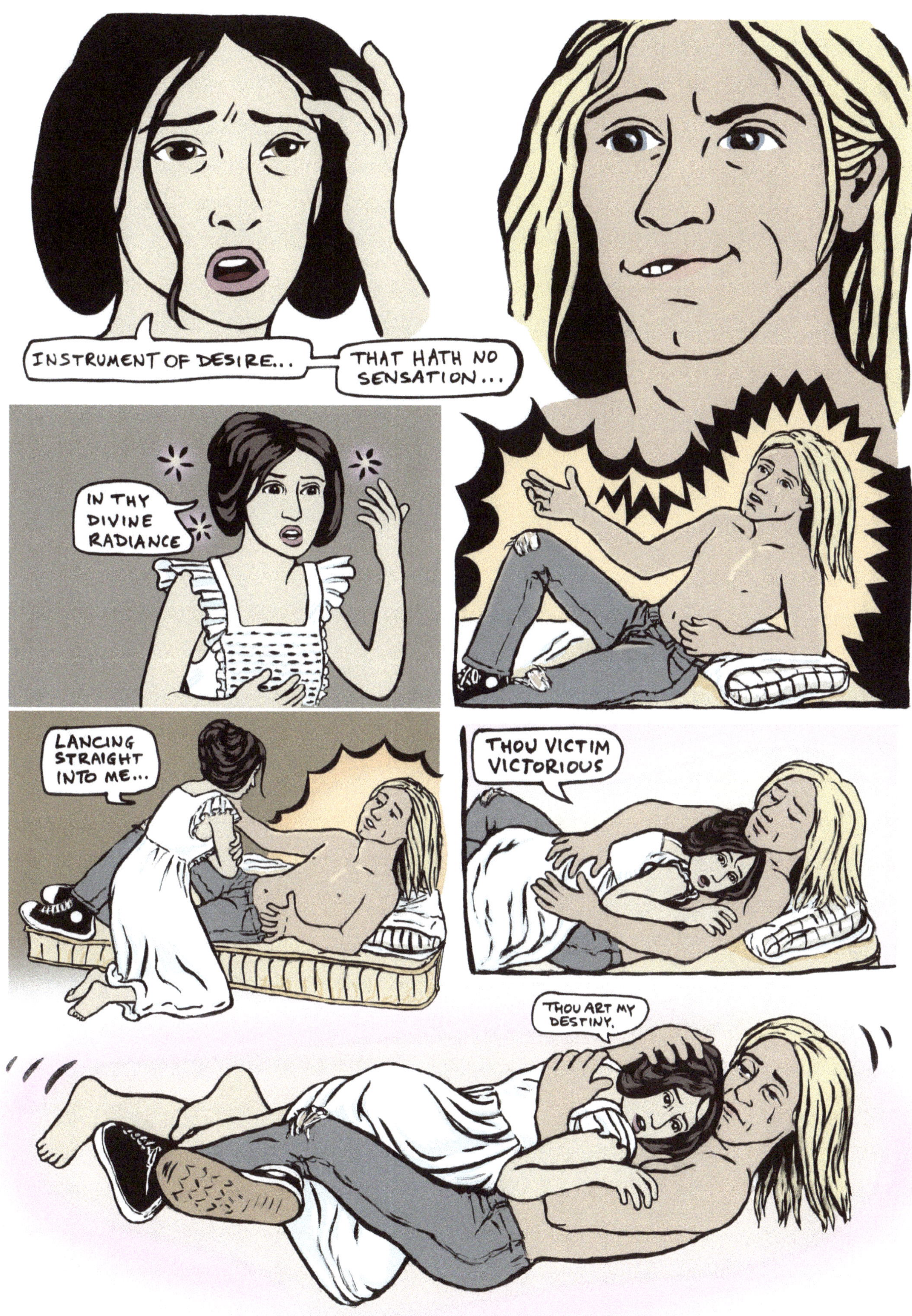
INSTRUMENT OF DESIRE...
THAT HATH NO SENSATION...
IN THY DIVINE RADIANCE
LANCING STRAIGHT INTO ME...
THOU VICTIM VICTORIOUS
THOU ART MY DESTINY.

WHOOOOOOSH!!
OHHHH!
FOOM
HA HA
HA HA

Charlotte must obey and she knows what to do. She lies down on his reclining body and his arms go around her. His body levitates slightly and then drops to the floor. As if this connects him with his power source, he now rises swiftly into the air, and Charlotte can see the lights of Manhattan twinkling in the distance.

" He'll fly right out that window," she imagines. "We are going to the city."

But to her surprise, they float into the hall and down the staircase.

The hotel is burning, but that's not what frightens Charlotte most as she clings to the boy's muscular shoulders. Already he seems older and stronger. He is now floating upright and carrying her in his arms.

"Oh, what is going to happen to me?" she wails. She is terrified by her own sexual excitement, by the surety that her dazzling captor cares nothing for her, by the anticipation of her own degradation.

They float through the lobby.

"They will imagine I'm a ghost" Charlotte thinks.

The lights have all gone out and people are talking nervously. The darkness is a harbinger of the fiery death that awaits them this night. A ghastly vision appears: a figure dressed in a long white gown, seated on a chair, floating across the room and out the door.

There is one short flight of stairs now between Charlotte's captor and the front door. As they float downwards Charlotte spies a tiny blonde girl about three years old standing on the steps, waving a speculum. The girl laughs an unearthly, childish laugh, and Charlotte shudders.

Outside the young man alights on the sidewalk and strides resolutely in the direction of the city, clutching Charlotte in his arms.

"He is taking me toward my destiny."

She is hopelessly in love with him already, but she tries not to think about the future.

Looking back, she sees a woman chasing after them, gaining on them. It seems to Charlotte that she is a witch, and a friend. She carries a chaplet in her hand.

"Maybe this won't be so bad after all," Charlotte muses to herself. "Maybe I'll be the beautiful princess..."

As if reading her thoughts, the youth speaks in an off-hand tone.

"No, actually, I'll turn you into a pig."

A **PIG**!?

Charlotte sighs, resigning herself to whatever may come.

Just then the woman in pursuit catches up to them, and thrusts the garland into Charlotte's hands. It is like a crown or a dreamcatcher, made of wires and red and purple ribbons, beads and flowers. A magical thing.

"We found this," the woman breathes. "It connects you with Bill. Rosetta with Bill. You with Rosetta—"

The youth leaps into the air with Charlotte in his arms, leaving the messenger behind.

"—But you can only use it once!" the woman calls as they take off. Examining the wreath, Charlotte notices several small watch faces dangling from it, ticking away.

Charlotte wakes up.

And so do I.

Scene v.

In Which Rosetta Awakens

...To record the vivid and electrifying nightmare in perfect detail in my journal.

YOU WANT TO QUIT YOUR JOB?!
I CAN FREELANCE!
I'LL HAVE MORE TIME FOR THE BAND—
AND MY ART, TOO.
IT'S AMAZING HOW STUPID I WAS.
MY GOD, I LEFT A GOOD JOB...
SET OUT ON A COURSE THAT WOULD WRECK MY ENTIRE LIFE...
ALL SO I COULD FOLLOW THE SIREN CALL OF MY OWN CREATIVE POWER!
AND ALL, HAD I ONLY KNOWN IT THEN, AT THE BIDDING OF A ROGUISH SPIRIT, ONE WHO HARDLY HAS MY B—
ZZZOIIING
DO YOU REGRET IT, THEN, ROSETTA?
I DON'T BELIEVE IN REGRET.
BUT IT SURE HAS BEEN A HARDER ROAD THAN I ONCE IMAGINED.
WELL, YOU'RE AN OPTIMIST.
AND I HAVE A PRETTY GOOD IMAGINATION!

NO, I DO STILL HAVE SOME DOUBTS; DID I DO THE RIGHT THING?
CREATING THIS F'D UP "MEMOIR"...
IS SUPPOSED TO HELP ME FIGURE THAT OUT, I GUESS.
HEY, KNOCK YOURSELF OUT. JUST HURRY UP AND GET TO MY PART OF THE STORY.
I'LL GET TO IT. I'LL GET TO IT.
YOU BELONG TO ME.
DON'T FORGET THAT!
≶SIGH≷
OK, FIRST OF ALL, THIS WASN'T THE BOOK I SET OUT TO MAKE.
IN FACT, AFTER FIVE YEARS OF THERAPY, I'D PUT ALL THE MADNESS BEHIND ME.
OH, I'VE TRIED TO IGNORE HIM, BE-LIEVE ME.
BUT IT SEEMS LIKE WHENEVER I FOCUS ON ANYTHING—
OTHER THAN HIS CHRONIC SATYRIASIS, HIS LATEST OBSESSION—
ANY SUCH DEPARTURE MEETS WITH SOME SORT OF DISASTER!
FINE. DO IT YOUR WAY.
I HAVE NOTHING BUT TIME.
GO AHEAD. HAVE A BLAME-FEST.
I'M USED TO IT!

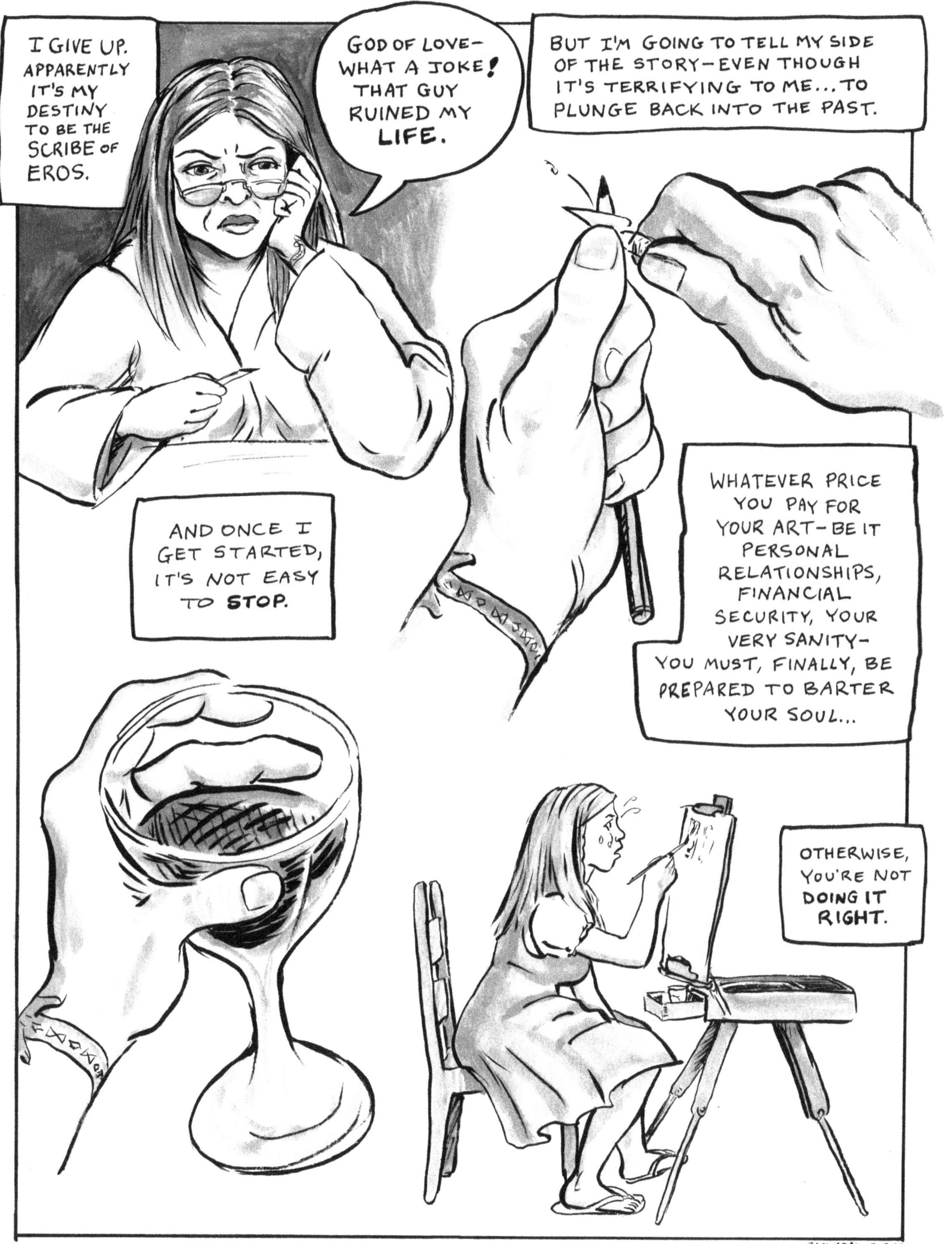
I GIVE UP. APPARENTLY IT'S MY DESTINY TO BE THE SCRIBE OF EROS.
GOD OF LOVE— WHAT A JOKE! THAT GUY RUINED MY LIFE.
BUT I'M GOING TO TELL MY SIDE OF THE STORY—EVEN THOUGH IT'S TERRIFYING TO ME...TO PLUNGE BACK INTO THE PAST.
AND ONCE I GET STARTED, IT'S NOT EASY TO STOP.
WHATEVER PRICE YOU PAY FOR YOUR ART—BE IT PERSONAL RELATIONSHIPS, FINANCIAL SECURITY, YOUR VERY SANITY— YOU MUST, FINALLY, BE PREPARED TO BARTER YOUR SOUL...
OTHERWISE, YOU'RE NOT DOING IT RIGHT.

Scene vi.

In Which a Monster Is Aroused

ACROPOLIS OF THE GODS
ON MOUNT OLYMPUS
c 2000 AD
N
DIONYSOS
POSEIDON
EROS
HADES
HEPHAISTOS
IRIS
HERMES
ZEUS
HERA
HESTIA
ARES
APHRODITE
ATHENA
ARTEMIS
APOLLO
DEMETER
HELIOS

I DON'T CARE FOR THESE SHOES ONE BIT!
careful—ow.

REALLY? I RATHER LIKE THEM.
nghk!
AND THE SLEEVES!
GOOD GOD—

HAVEN'T I BEEN HUMILIATED ENOUGH?!
WHAT!?
HUMILIATED?

HA HA HA HA! LOOSEN UP AND RELAX, BABY!!
EVERYTHING'S COOL...
AND BESIDES,
WE'RE ALONE NOW.

—BUT HE'LL BE BACK DIRECTLY,
WINCE? HE WON'T MIND IF—

DON'T!
COME ON, BABY!
IT'S OUR HONEYMOON!
WHUMMMM

THIS IS THE WAAY THE LAADY RIDES...
LAADY RIDES...
LAADEE RIDES!
I'D — I'D JUST —
JUST PRE —
FER TO — TO WEAR —
SOMETHING —AANNGH!
THIS IS THE WAAY
THE LAADY RIDES —
SOMETHING — OH! OHH!
TROTTITY — TROTTITY TROT!
OH! OH! OH!
A LITTLE — UH!
LESS — NG! — RE —
VEAL — ING!
OH. WHAT DID YOU HAVE IN MIND —
A NUN'S HABIT?

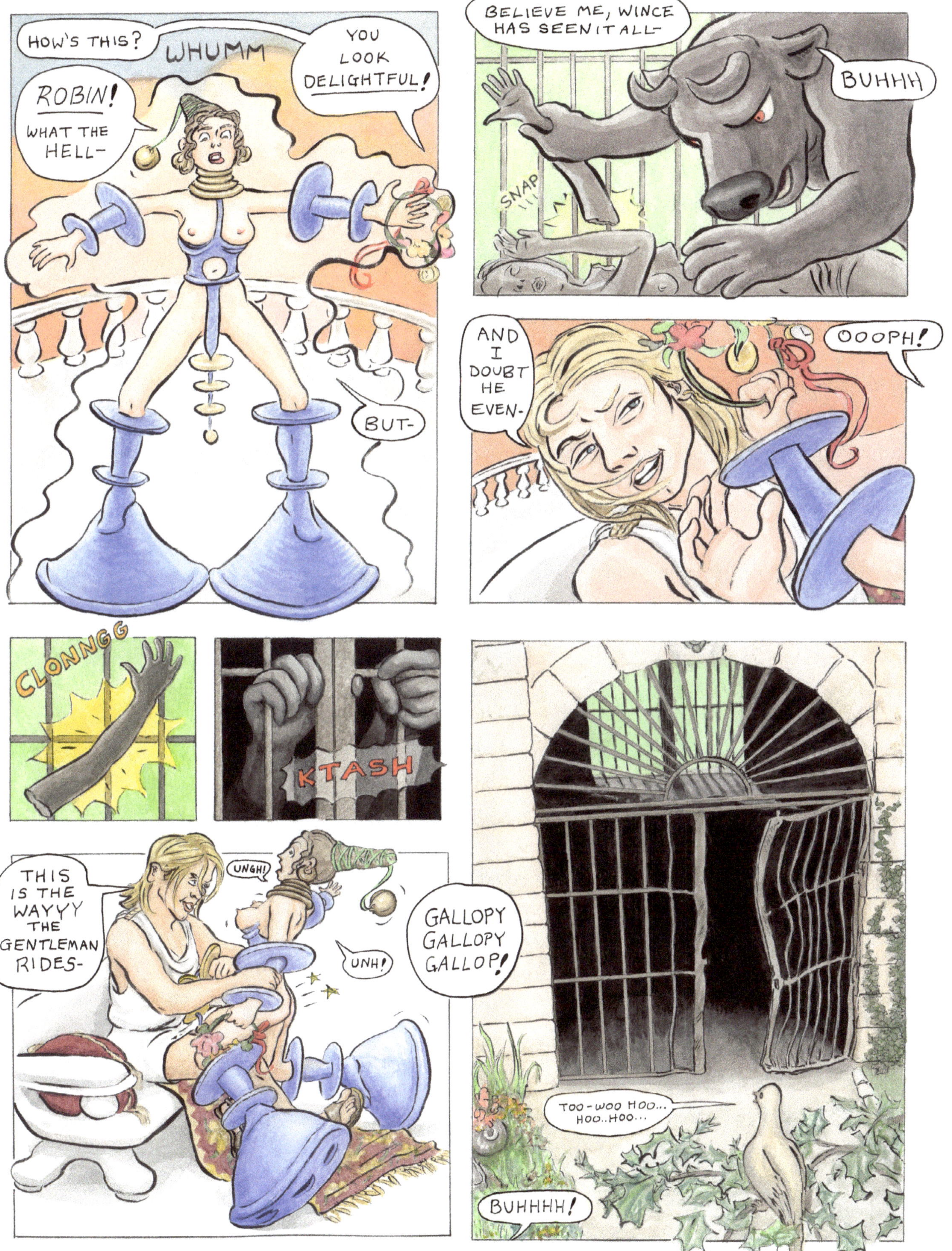

HOW'S THIS?
WHUMM
YOU LOOK DELIGHTFUL!
ROBIN! WHAT THE HELL—
BUT—
BELIEVE ME, WINCE HAS SEEN IT ALL—
BUHHH
SNAP
AND I DOUBT HE EVEN—
OOOPH!
CLONNGG
KTASH
THIS IS THE WAYYY THE GENTLEMAN RIDES—
UNGH!
UNH!
GALLOPY GALLOPY GALLOP!
TOO-WOO HOO... HOO..HOO...
BUHHHH!

Scene vii.

In Which Rosetta Receives a Message

Rosetta paused at the door to her studio, fingers on the light switch, and looked around at the enormous, inviting space. Less than a year ago it had been a grimy warren filled with dilapidated shelving. She'd recognized the potential beauty of the space instantly. *It's a cathedral for art,* she'd told Angel.

She gazed now with satisfaction at the sparkling floors and pillars of polished wood, the enormous arched windows framing the winking tree that presided, resplendent, over the wide canal below.

Rosetta was filled up with peanut butter and banana fudge pie baked by her new friend Francie for the charity sale. She had consumed a measure of brandy-spiked cider. A stack of letters for Amnesty International was nestled in her handbag, ready to be posted in the morning. And she had earned fifty-six dollars and twenty-five cents for Doctors Without Borders. Not bad for a bunch of threadbare artists.

Across the spacious room, pinned to the wood paneling, was an expanse of paper upon which comic book pages were rendered at an unusually large size. She had started out at 18"x24" plus two inch borders, but the figures, rendered in calligraphic black lines, had a tendency to burst out of the frames and consume all the available space around them. Her eyes fell on the faces of the characters, Robin aka the god Eros, and Charlotte Eyre, the older woman he had pursued in her dream. Robin leered at Charlotte with a twisted grin. Charlotte stared icily back at him, her mouth open and spouting prickly poetry. In another frame, Robin seized her thumb, his knife poised to cut the pad.

These semaphores from her subconscious were as vivid now in her mind's eye as on the morning twelve years before, when she jotted the dream into her journal.

Why would anyone ever want to read this bizarre story? she wondered. And yet she felt an urgency to record it.

A twinge of dismay marred her contentment as she contemplated her interrupted work. It had been a month since she'd picked up a brush.

"Ready to go?" Angel asked. "Do you have your phone and your keys?"

Following Angel up Route 202, she prayed the electricity would be back on when they got home to Pelham.

As she drove between bent and rimed oaks and maples, a huge meteor appeared from the left, streaked across the star-frosted sky and vanished behind a black silhouette of trees. At the same instant her car radio turned itself on.

"...Traffic and weather on the ones. And up next on Ten-Ten Wins, it's the sports report brought to you by..."

Puzzling, that the radio had come on by itself, and that she was picking up a New York City station. How far away was that transmitter? She'd never been able to

tune in much above New Haven, and they were eighty miles further north than that.

She switched the radio off, then on again. Weird.

She turned it back off. A few minutes later, it came on again in a burst of static. Seamus, Rosetta's cream-colored toy poodle, ensconced in the passenger seat beside her, let out a plaintive whine.

She turned the dial back to the off position, and drove on through ghostly ice sculptures. A minute or two went by, then the radio switched on for a third time.

Rosetta felt around under the dog for her cell phone and dialed Angel.

"Hi, what's up?"

"Angel… are you experiencing any… strange phenomena?"

"I don't know what you mean."

"Did you see the meteor?"

"No."

"Well there was a great big one– and then my radio turned itself on!"

"Huh!" he said serenely.

"Angel, see if you can get Ten-Ten Wins." He obediently turned his radio on.

"Yup. I've got it."

"Isn't that bizarre though? I mean, you can't get that station up here."

"Really? I never noticed."

"Look! Another shooting star! Maybe it has something to do with the meteor shower," she said, grasping for a scientific explanation. "It's a cold, clear night, which is probably good for reception. Anyway there must be an unusual level of electromagnetic activity out there."

"I guess so," said Angel.

Rosetta clicked off the phone. A minute or two later, her radio turned itself on again: Ten-Ten Wins, from way down south of there.

She was getting spooked. She couldn't help feeling that someone or something was sending her a message. But that was silly.

She thought about all those hundreds of square miles up ahead– the ice storm had knocked out electricity in parts of three states– where everything was shrouded in ice. Acres of prisms, a mass of crystals that were amplifying the sound waves. That had to be it. The forest up ahead had been transformed into a vast radio set.

An atmospheric effect, and extremem weather phenomenon.

When they got home the electricity was back on, and with it the water pump. They showered and went gratefully to bed.

"I'm setting the alarm for five-thirty," Angel announced, poking at his handset. Rosetta was due to catch a train at 7:10 out of Springfield.

It was difficult to get to sleep. The ice on the metal roof, melted by the heat rising from inside the house, dripped down the icicles that had formed along the eaves

and fell with a constant loud drumming on the air conditioner outside the window. However Rosetta eventually slipped into a deep sleep, and dreamed.

She and Phoebe were in an elevator. Phoebe was a girl she'd once shared a cabin with in high school church camp, Rosetta recalled: a big talker with braces, horn-rimmed glasses and a perfect figure. Phoebe claimed the distinction of being the first of the Jesus nerds in their cabin to have relinquished her virginity.

Camp was like a week-long slumber party. Late at night the girls would gather 'round Phoebe to soak up every juicy detail about her romance with Ben, her trekkie boyfriend.

"So I was knitting some baby booties as a gift for my cousin, who was expecting," Phoebe recounted one night, "when Ben walked in.

" 'What are you making?' he said, and I said, 'booties!' " The word came out halfway between a chirp and a squeal.

"You should have seen his face! He was white as a sheet, and he went like this: 'B-b-b-booties?' "

The circle of girls listened with breathless envy. The *that* was power! How the boy cowered before the awesome hegemony of the fertile womb!

It was an epiphany. Rosetta was determined to lose her virginity as soon as it could be arranged.

Riding the elevator now with Phoebe and some others, Rosetta knew, as one knew in dreams, that they were in a building belonging to a wealthy man, a glamorous playboy. Phoebe was determined to meet him. She knew about a special button that would allow entree into the private floors. As teh elevator rose, she pressed it, and a section of the floor slid open.

The trapdoor was only open for a few seconds. Rosetta watched Phoebe disappear but hesitated, not wanting to fall.

She had missed her chance, but she had been watching Phoebe. The elevator proceeded up to another floor and passengers got on and off. Rosetta pushed the secret button, and a gap opened in the upper third of the elevator wall, opposite the door. She stepped toward it and was immediately drawn through.

Next thing she knew, a conveyor belt was carrying her along in a vast, grey interior. She felt as though she were on an amusement park ride. She could see Phoebe in the distance, reclining in a revealing negligee. Phoebe pored over a fanzine about the rich playboy, as the rubbery causeway moved her along.

Off in the nondescript gloom there whirled a contraption that looked a bit like a Ferris wheel. Rosetta recognized it as the "spanking machine" in the bathtub game she used to play with her sisters when they were little girls. They had all been so innocent, but oh, how the bubbly foam had spattered the walls, with a spankity-spank!

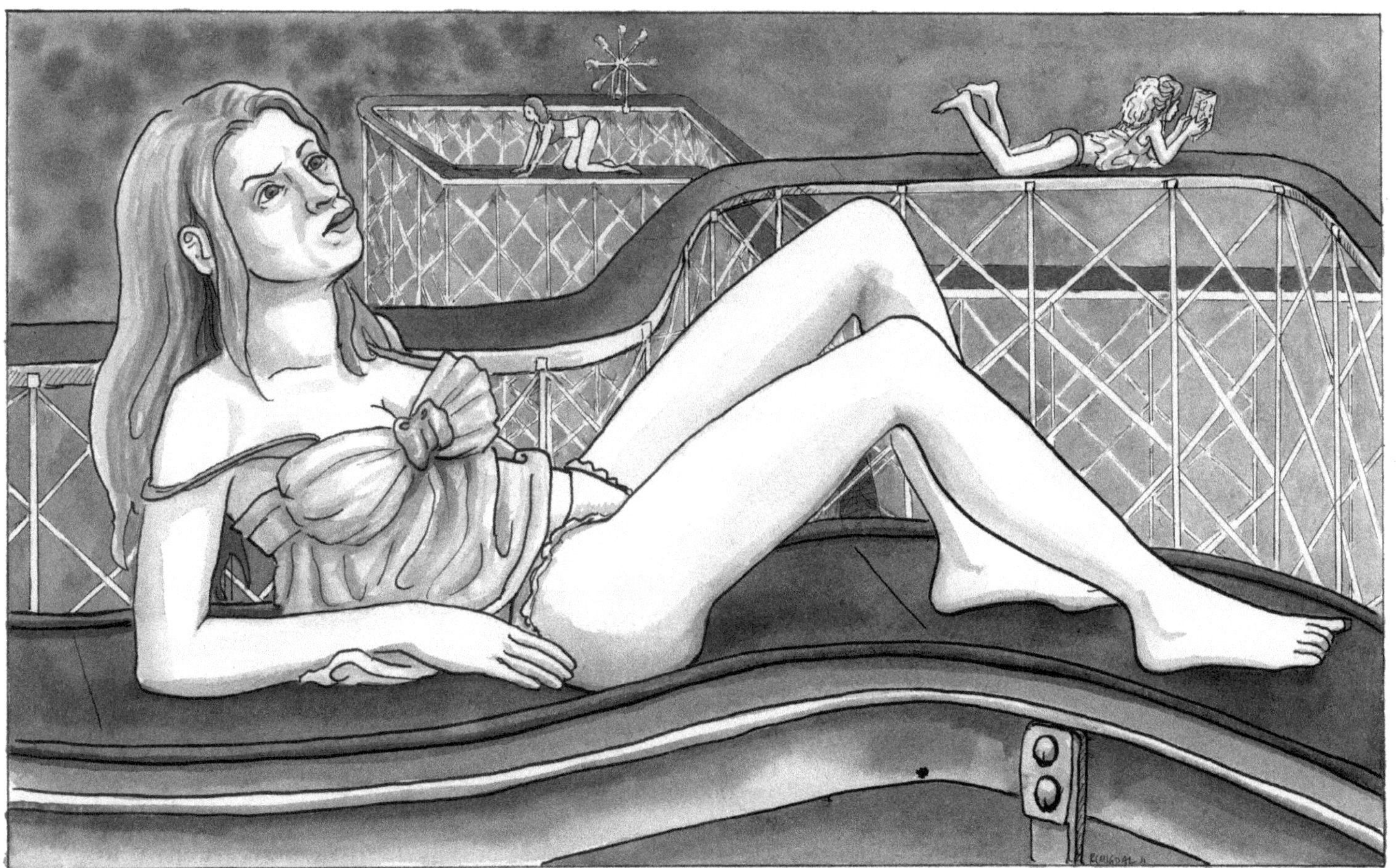

Transported willy nilly toward who knew where, all in a state of luxuriant undress, her bottom began to ache and tingle.

Now Rosetta came to another chamber. Here the face of the rich playboy appeared before her as if in a hologram. He was a man of perfect features, clean-shaven and with shoulder length, fair hair. His visage contained all the arrogance of power, beauty and brilliant charm. He gazed at her seductively, embodying all desire.

Rosetta was unmoved by this, knowing it to be artifice.

He smiled and his face was radiant, warm and alluring. *Au contraire*, he seemed to be telling her, *I am a very sincere guy*. His approval was a thing to be basked in, he seemed to imply, a balm and an aegis.

Suddenly his visage changed and he looked upon her with searing scorn. Rosetta understood that she was now being rejected sexually.

Again, she felt no emotion. The conveyor moved on, taking Rosetta with it. She looked back and saw that the wealthy Don Juan was not a hologram at all. He was still standing there, his trousers around his ankles, his manhood at attention. He was following her with his eyes, with searching interest.

Apparently she had made a powerful impression on him. Much more than Phoebe had, sycophantic fangirl that she was, Rosetta thought, feeling smug.

The next room was of intermediate size, accommodating a counter or row of tables around the periphery, with space behind them; it was arranged like a laboratory, or a series of displays in a science fair. Rosetta was conveyed along until she reached a large transparent box, in which a liquor bottle stood. A tube led from the top of the bottle to a flask, and a clear liquid continually bubbled from the liquor bottle into the flask.

A man stood behind this display, dressed in a sort of sleeveless jumpsuit that displayed his muscular arms.

"Alcohol is your issue," the man said. He was stern and pragmatic: just the facts, ma'am.

Rosetta was swept along faster now around the room, stopping at none of the other stations. There was no sign of Phoebe.

At the end of the circuit Rosetta approached the door by which she came in. There stood the rich playboy, but this was the porcelain Ken-doll version, or else he was clad in a form-fitting white unitard. Over his belly she saw a vignette, the small silhouette of a figure in lotus position. Inside this figure was a strip covered in what appeared to be Hindu script.

Rosetta now understood that she had passed some sort of test and reached a higher level of consciousness. But it appeared that the examination was not over yet.

"Are you ready for the book?" The blond man asked her, though his mouth did not speak.

"I will read the book," she replied.

He gazed at her with a look of anxiety and pain. This was not the answer he wanted.

It seemed to Rosetta that she could hear his voice in her head, saying, "Are you committed to following the path?"

And she knew that he meant not only that she was to read the book, but also to record what was written there.

Rosetta thought to herself, "I am not a child."

She returned his look steadily and then, wishing only to reassure him, she leaned over and embraced him.

He pulled away, visibly shaken, as her bosom pressed against him. Rosetta knew him at last.

"It's Robin!"

It appeared that she was not the only one who was being tested, and taught, in this place.

"So that's your issue," she said gently.

"Well, you have got quite a rack," he admitted. "It's hard for me not to think about it."

"It's attached to my body," Rosetta pointed out. "It goes where I go."

Suddenly she was outside the building, soaring through the air somewhere above midtown Manhattan, and descending rapidly. Soon she was floating above the sidewalk, and as she landed gently on the pavement she realized that she was wearing her bathrobe, and had no shoes on. The sidewalk was littered with small stones

SUDDENLY...

I'LL NEVER GET TO BROOKLYN ON FOOT!
BUT THAT'S ALL RIGHT...
I CAN FLY!

UP... UP... UP...!

and here and there, broken glass. After a few steps she knew she couldn't walk back to Brooklyn this way.

"That's OK, I can fly," she said to herself. She rose into the air and began to zoom forward. She knew that she would need to rise up above the buildings and trees to get there quickly and without running into obstacles and mishaps. Gaining altitude was sometimes pretty difficult for her, but she felt that she could do it. Rosetta closed her eyes and willed herself upward, and when she opened them she was above the city.

"I'm on my way," she thought happily.

Again she was instantly transported, this time to a shining boat in a harbor.

She stood on the floating wooden dock beside a yacht, presumably belonging to Robin, and she suspected that he was around somewhere. Rosetta was becoming annoyed at being sent hither and yon like this. First she'd been put out on the street barefoot, and then brought to this fancy boat–what did he think he was he doing? Anyway, at the moment she was determined to get to her son Antoine's place. It was inconceivable to go to Brooklyn without seeing him.

Seamus pattered toward her along the dock. Another of Robin's little tricks: if she were going to fly home, she would need to carry the little poodle. She wasn't sure she'd be able to gain enough altitude with the extra weight.

She climbed up a white gangway with a steel banister, thinking she could take to the air more easily from that height. She called Seamus and took him in her arms, but she wasn't able to take off.

Rosetta looked down at the clear, blue-green water of the small harbor, and realized that it terminated in a waterfall on the far side. All she had to do was swim or wade across the shallow pool, which was warm and inviting, and she might be able to get up enough speed, when she and Seamus passed over the waterfall, to take to the air. She wasn't convinced she could pull it off, and she was a bit worried about having to swim with the poodle in her arms, but she plunged into the water and began to move steadily ahead.

"And then I woke up," Rosetta concluded.

"That's quite a dream," Angel said gently, gunning the old Volvo up a broad curve on Interstate 91. "It looks like we'll get to the Springfield station with five minutes to spare," he added.

As they topped the Holyoke range the reddish dawn bled from behind the black pines. The rising sun was heralded by a distinct column of brilliant orange. The apparition spearing through a galleon of clouds took the form of a thick mast, with vermilion sails spread above. Or, Rosetta thought, a phallus rising in the East.

It was a sundog, a refraction phenomenon caused by ice crystals in the atmosphere, not a portent, a communication from the gods. It would be absurd to think so.

Scene viii.

In Which the Tale of Asterion is Told

Legend does not paint Asterion as a profound thinker.

In myth the Minotaur is trapped in his Labyrinth simply because he is too dim-witted to find his way out. He is bested by the "clever" Theseus, with the assistance of Ariadne, who is the real brains behind the operation.

The truth is that Asterion had no desire to escape.

The bull-headed boy had no wish to walk among the lords and ladies in the sunlit colonnades of Knossos. The subterranean chambers where he wandered in timeless darkness suited his gloomy character. He did not care for conversation, could not bear the looks of pity and disgust that he detected in the eyes of other highborn youths at the palace.

As a child he had spent his golden hours in the alleyways of the town below, hiding among fleets of billowing skirts hanging out to dry, where baskets were his warships, and a pottery stall became a towering fortress for the plunder; an imaginary land where he, Asterion, was king.

But even his former haunts at his nurse's house near the market now offered little in the way of temptations. The smell of sizzling beef made him feel rather ill, and he recoiled from the thought of the food shops, with their skewers of roasted meats.

Contrary to legend, Asterion was a vegetarian, preferring grains and fresh grasses, salads and fruits. His mother the queen personally oversaw his diet, making sure he was daily brought baskets filled with the finest provisions, prepared to his taste. At his request these baskets were lowered into the chamber of the blue stalactites through a hole in the roof of the cave.

So Asterion saw no-one, except on holidays when the sacrificial combatants were sent in, one by one.

Asterion had uncanny night vision, and with his enormous nose, sensitive ears and titanic strength, he had every advantage over his puny adversaries. His usual strategy was to lie in wait at a particular turn in the passage near the underground spring. They always came that way sooner or later. Surprising his victim, he quickly disarmed the lout, then crushed the life out of him with his bare hands.

Asterion felt nothing but contempt for the warriors who brandished their spears and shouted his name in challenge. Braggarts and bullies filled him with dis-

taste.

But he didn't always kill them. Sometimes they were sharp-eared and quick, and stayed out of his way.

His sister knew this. It irritated Asterion that Ariadne seemed to think he needed looking after. He had little trouble ridding himself of unwanted guests. He suspected that the princess was secretly advising the champions to surrender at once upon entering his holy shrine, tossing their swords and spears into the pit of Rhea. Those who paid her heed stood some chance of being released unscathed at sunrise.

Never once had he been bested in a contest of strength and ferocity. Those who entered the twisted corridors of Arkalochori eager for battle were never seen again.

But to tell the truth, if he perceived no threat, the Minotaur soon tired of the chase and went to sleep.

For he was no showman, no bull dancer prancing about to impress the watching ladies. None could have compelled him to enter the arena, not even a hundred men.

Cowardice had nothing to do with it. The crisp snap of the pennants in the wind, the barks of bets being placed, and the thunder of the crowd urging him on to brutal feats of savagery–these were scenes that crowded his imagination as he crouched in the gloom, listening to the panicked gasps of his latest victim.

But the smells of the palace were sickening and strange to him now, and the bright glare of the sun only blinded him.

No, the crunch of a spine in his hands was sweeter in the dark.

One time he sliced open his forearm on a splinter of broken bone. After that, his mother had ordered a new suit of armor to be made for him, with gold-inlaid greaves, arm guards and a studded breastplate.

With such fine protective gear Asterion felt nearly invincible.

His father king Minos appreciated the strategic value of having so monstrous a son, and kept him well supplied with tender maidens exacted from the cities of the empire as tribute.

When a new girl was brought in, often dressed as Europa, the priestesses entered in a torchlit procession, carrying ceremonial objects: axes, garlands and wine. Ah, the taste of terror on his tongue was sweet, the soft flesh delicious to knead and rend: a pleasure of the senses that never failed to satisfy. This vice of his would have been frowned upon in the light of day. But deep in the maze, where none could hear or see, Asterion could indulge in his favorite pastime in peace.

All in all, Asterion mused wistfully, it had been a good life, back in the day: his salad days, his reign of terror in the Labyrinth.

No mortal warrior could ever have beaten him. This was one thought frequently replayed in the dull recesses of his mind, century after century. Dwelling upon his invincibility brought on the fantasies of his prowess in other departments. Then he would savor again his recollections of the women whose plump bodies had satiated his violent lusts in days of old. The deaths of the unlucky maidens had done nothing to erase their charms from his memory, serving rather as a testament to the awesome destructive power of his manly weapon.

No, Asterion was not prone to contemplation of the cosmos during the millenia

of his entombment in a casing of stone. His trammeled mind turned on the same top-
ics that had occupied it during his more active days.

One matter that irked him was that Theseus continued to be celebrated as the
author of his demise. It had been a mere coincidence that the Athenian Prince had
entered the sacred caves on the unluckiest day of Asterion's life.

Theseus had been told where to find a torch and flint, and had busied himself
raiding the treasure chamber of gold and silver offerings. But on the way back, he
had stumbled into Asterion.

"If the Athenians had seen the look on Theseus' face when he dropped those
ornamental hatchets and ran, they never would have believed his story," the Minotaur told himself.

But the lie that concealed the Prince's cowardice had stuck. Theseus had en-
sured this by abandoning Ariadne, the only soul who knew the true story, on a bar-
ren island during the boat ride home.

Theseus had claimed a kingdom and immortal fame. Meanwhile it was Asterion's fate to relive, over and over, the fateful moment when Pan turned him into a
marble statue.

Asterion had been in the chamber of the glowing walls, lunging at a shapely

captive when Pan, in a shocking invasion of his privacy, had popped up out of nowhere and transformed both Minotaur and victim into a frozen tableau of stone. Thus Asterion's unfortunate consort was blessed with a painless exit.

But the bovine-headed grandson of Zeus was a demigod, and could not die.

The travertine figures of monster and maid stood in their eternal pose for an hour or so before Theseus arrived to loot the treasury and claim Ariadne's clandestine dowry. Then, only minutes after the Athenian's terrified departure, the statues moved: they trembled, then wobbled. Dirt fell on them, then rocks and huge boulders landed to one side and another. It was the end of the world.

Centuries passed. Finally Asterion was unearthed by treasure hunters, and sold to a Roman merchant. The Minotaur and his bride came to adorn the atrium of Tetreus Pontificus, citizen of Pompeii. There Asterion was the envy of the neighborhood. Word of the dramatic, astonishingly realistic "sculpture" spread, and the house of Pontificus was visited by no less than three Empresses in ten years.

Asterion the statue had survived much and travelled far. At last his years in Pompeii, spent listlessly ignoring the gossip of the wives of wealthy traders, came to a catastrophic end. But just as Vesuvius spewed its deadly vomit over the peristyle, the Minotaur vanished from the earth.

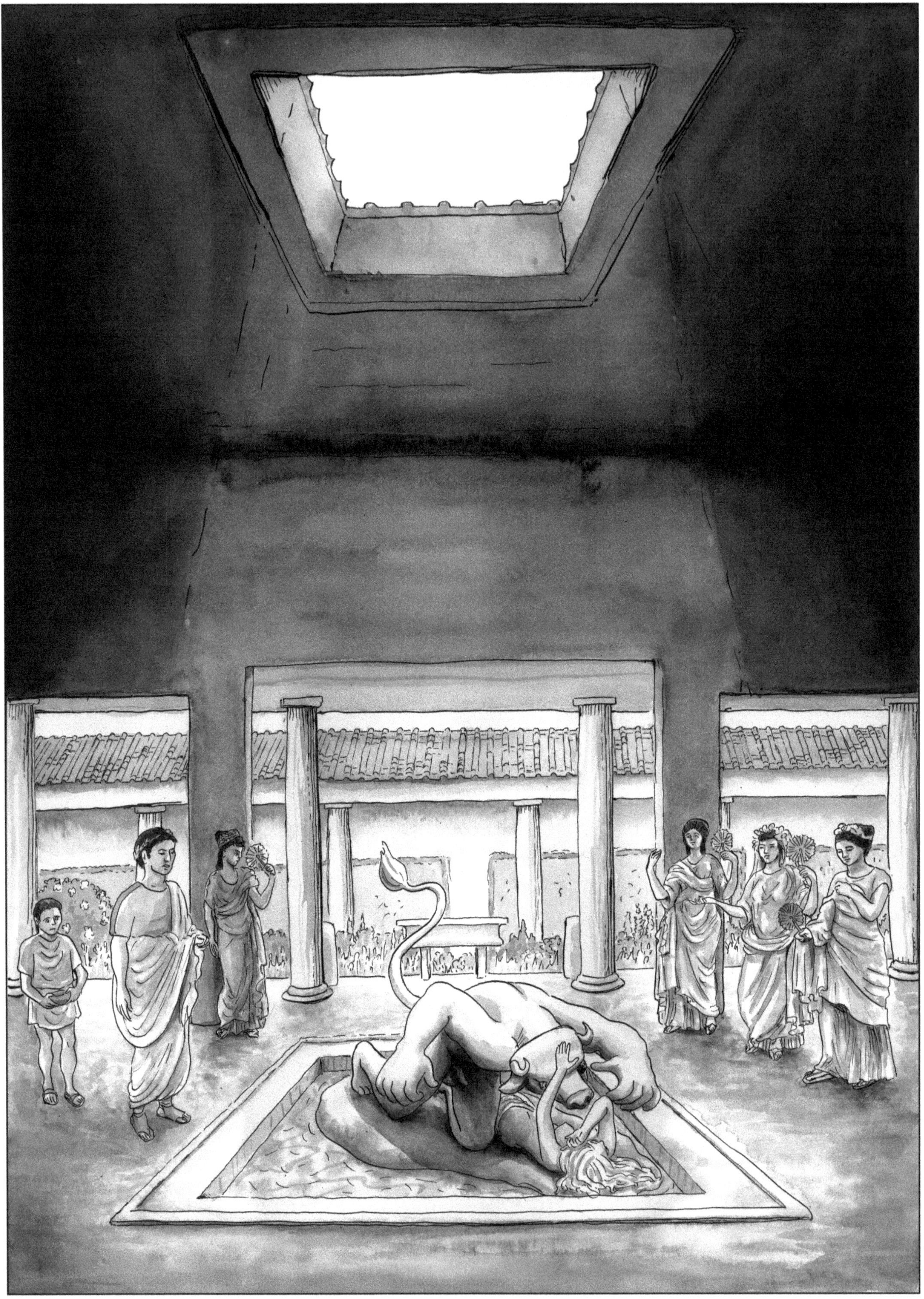

As Vesuvius' pall rains death upon the Bay of Naples, Eros looks down from on high.
NAPOLI
HERCVLANEVM
PLINY
POMPEII

SMASH!
THUNK!

BOUNCE
HECATE'S MUSTACHE!
WHAT SORT OF STATUE IS THIS?

It so happened that the God of Love, being devoted to the arts, was loath to permit any masterpiece to perish in a cataclysm of nature or war. Whenever possible, he arranged to spirit away such works as caught his fancy, to be housed forever more in the vast galleries on his estate.

And that is how Asterion came into Cupid's possession. Recognizing the true nature of his acquisition, Eros took the precaution of enclosing the statue in a locked and barred storage area below his private porch. And there the Minotaur was left to fume eternity away in motionless rage.

Pan. That damned Satyr had destroyed him! But why?

Taking the girl for himself could not have been his object. But puzzling over Pan's motive only made Asterion's head throb.

He turned the bloodshot glare of his mind's eye to thoughts of revenge. For the Minotaur possessed creativity of a sort, which he employed in fantasizing infinite ways of maiming and dismembering the horned god. These imaginary scenarios might have played out indefinitely in the recesses of the imprisoned monster's brain, but for the arrival of a visitor.

To the iron gate of the cage there came one day unannounced the deity Apollo. Words were whispered then, that planted the seed of a new obsession in Asterion's dark mind.

Centuries passed.

And then the hour came when, in the light of an eternal sunset, Charlotte was brought to Olympus. That very hour life began to stir anew in the breast of Asterion.

Who or what was the agent of this reawakening? I will leave it to you, dear Reader, to draw your own conclusions.

But whatever it was that woke the beast, awaken he did.

Scene ix.

In Which a Monster is Unleashed

UNBELIEVABLE!

YOU EGOTISTICAL... SELFISH...
BASTARD!
ERATO
BUHHH...

BUUUUHHHH....

At last he was free, and the Minotaur did not stop to smell the roses. He had been sniffing flowers for long enough, there in his cage, imprisoned in a sleeve of stone. What he desired now, with a fiery urgency, was to impale, to violate and ravage and devour, every sylph on Olympos. He would surely find any number of them near at hand, here in the Gardens of Cupid. How long they had tormented him with their giggles and frolics he did not know, but now his vengeance would be swift.

Drawn by the sound of girlish laughter, Asterion approached a fountain surrounded by potted trees. Lurking behind the foliage, he saw there a group of nymphs at play. One of the delicious maidens was bound in silken cords, a bandage tied around her eyes. Her playmates surrounded her, preparing her for a sensual initiation into the sweet rites of the sacred maidens, anointing her curvaceous body with oil.

Without further hesitation Asterion lunged at the group of nymphs. The closest one knelt at the edge of the marble basin, and he seized her. Instantly, however, she transformed herself into an oleander tree, defeating his lustful purpose.

The inflamed Minotaur bellowed a curse and, whirling toward the others, he decided that he had better choose a likely victim from among sylphs, and take her prisoner. The redhead in bondage was the easiest target.

Some of the nymphs had scattered, but others faced him bravely as he leaped forward to take possession of the voluptuous peri. She did not yet comprehend the nature of her peril, and made not move to escape. He snatched up the blindfolded girl, ripping her from the arms of her screaming playfellows.

The nude nymph squirmed and cried out for her friends. Asterion clapped a hand over her mouth, flung aside an attacking nymph, and clutched his booty under his arm he carried her off. She kicked wildly, but remained in her feminine form, for she was not yet an initiate of the magic arts. The triumphant monster loped away rapidly, seeking for a secluded spot where he could indulge in the brutal defilement of his prize. Her soft body and the smell of her terror filled him with unholy lust. There must, he thought, be a remote grove or cavern somewhere in this pleasure garden, where he could ravish the maiden at his leisure, unmolested by any interference.

And where was Robin, the lord of this palace, who ought to be overseeing, protecting and defending the nymphs in these gardens? Away above, he too was bent on taking his pleasure in the charms of an unwilling captive. He had so far strayed from his own principles, as to lose himself in the single-minded pursuit and seduction of a woman whose favors had long been denied him. And now that he had her in his power, he was unable to resist taking advantage of her condition in a way that he himself, in saner mind, would certainly have deplored.

Dear Reader, well may you judge him harshly. To what extent were the crimes of Eros to blame for the chaos that now descended upon his sanctuary? His guilt will be determined in the coming volumes.

For now, let us draw a curtain on this regrettable scene, and say adieu.